CRADLE BOOK

Stories & Fables

CRADLE BOOK

Stories & Fables

by Craig Morgan Teicher

AMERICAN READER SERIES, No. 13

BOA EDITIONS, LTD. • ROCHESTER, NY • 2010

First Edition
10 11 12 13   7 6 5 4 3 2 1

For information about permission to reuse any material from this book please
contact The Permissions Company at www.permissionscompany.com or e-mail
permdude@eclipse.net.

Publications by BOA Editions, Ltd.—a not-for-profit corporation under section 501
(c) (3) of the United States Internal Revenue Code—are made possible with funds
from a variety of sources, including public funds from the New York State Council
for the Arts, a state agency; the Literature Program of the National Endowment for
the Arts; the County of Monroe, NY; the Lannan Foundation for support of the
Lannan Translations Selection Series; the Sonia Raiziss Giop Charitable Foundation;
the Mary S. Mulligan Charitable Trust; the Rochester Area Community Foundation; the Arts & Cultural Council for Greater Rochester; the Steeple-Jack Fund;
the Ames-Amzalak Memorial Trust in memory of Henry Ames, Semon Amzalak
and Dan Amzalak; the TCA Foundation; and contributions from many individuals
nationwide. See Colophon on page 72 for special individual acknowledgments.

Cover Design: Sandy Knight
Front Cover Art: "The Artificial Horizon" by Matthea Harvey
Back Cover Art: "Fortune Otherwise Known as Time" by Matthea Harvey
Interior Design and Composition: Bill Jones
Manufacturing: McNaughton & Gunn
BOA Logo: Mirko

Library of Congress Cataloging-in-Publication Data

Teicher, Craig Morgan, 1979-
Cradle book : stories & fables / by Craig Morgan Teicher. -- 1st ed.
p. cm. — (American reader series ; no. 13)
Includes bibliographical references and index.
ISBN 978-1-934414-35-4 (pbk. : alk. paper)
I. Title.
PS3620.E4359C73 2010
813'.6--dc22
                            2009028302

This book is for Cal

CONTENTS

III. from *The Book of Sleep*

THIS STORY

This story is older than the words with which it was written, though this is the first time it has ever been told.

I. from *The Book of Silence*

THE GROANING COWS

One night, as if responding to some invisible signal, all the cows began groaning. They groaned and groaned all the next day and did not stop at nightfall. This went on for days and days. No one could sleep. The children were becoming more and more afraid. Nearly driven mad, everyone in town gathered in the meeting hall.

Were the cows sick? Was it a warning? Of what? What should they do? No one could agree. Someone suggested that perhaps there was something wrong with the grass, and the cows were groaning because their stomachs ached. But this did not seem likely as the other animals ate the same grass and none of them were groaning. Someone else wondered whether the cows had finally tired of their servitude. Perhaps their groaning was a cry for freedom. But no one else was willing to believe that cows had such ideas. No one could think of a good explanation, and no one could think what to do, so they agreed to meet again in one week's time.

Still the cows continued to groan, night and day, while the farmers milked them, while they were being led out to pasture, when it was dark outside and they should have slept. Their voices never tired of groaning.

After a week had passed the town gathered again, and the mayor said that something must be done. He determined that all the cows in town must be slaughtered. Then he would go to the next town and buy more cows with the money set aside for the harvest festival, which they would have to do without this year. Since no one could think of a better idea, the people of the town agreed.

That night, all the men met in the square. They brought with them every tool of violence they had—scythes and clubs, knives and picks and rakes—so no one would be without a weapon. Then, holding torches, the mob made its way to the first farm. They would all kill the cows together.

As they reached the place where the groaning cows were standing, the cows seemed to take no notice of their approach, despite the glint of the torches on the blades the men carried. In truth, the men were nervous, still unsure whether they were truly taking the best course, but the mayor was among them, and he urged them on. They raised their weapons and prepared to strike.

Just then a girl ran into their path and stood between the men and the cows. She was the weaver's daughter, a quiet girl who kept rabbits and loved to make up songs.

"Stop!" she cried. "You must not kill these cows, or else terrible luck will befall us all!" Then she put her hand on the soft muzzle of the nearest cow. To her surprise, and to the surprise of everyone there, as she touched it, the cow stopped groaning. Soon all of the cows were quiet, and precious silence filled the night. Everyone went home and slept for what seemed like the first time in their lives.

The next night, just as the sun finally set, all the pigs began groaning, as if responding to some invisible signal. They groaned and groaned and would not stop.

The poor weaver's daughter. She knew then, when she heard the groaning, that her life would never be her own. It would belong to the pigs and the cows, to the goats and the ducks, to the hens and the rabbits. Most of all, it would belong to the men, whom she knew would never let her be.

THE PRISONER

I am telling the truth, though that is of little consequence to my captors. It is not the truth that they hope to force from my lips.

And they will get what they want—certainly they will, because I can only endure so much, like anyone—but not yet. For now, I still have the will to resist.

First, I will make them abandon all dignity, pride and restraint as they torture me. By remaining silent, I will make them do the unthinkable, even if the price to pay is that I must suffer it.

For I have already told them the truth: that we are all capable of anything, any merciless act. They would not believe me. Once they prove I am right, I will tell them the lie they want to hear: that there are some things we will not do.

THE REWARD

For his good deeds, he will be granted one wish, and so he will wish to be invisible. Those who had always seen him—and he does not put much stock in this group, for they seem to him a lonely and motley band who are used to being ignored by everyone but themselves—will no longer see him, and those who had never seen him, or who had never paid any attention if they had, but whose attention he most craves, will now not be able to detect his longing glances.

So he will go through the world mostly undetected, except perhaps as a passing breeze or a ghost haunting its old bed, edging the new sleeper out. Perhaps the animals will see him—no one really knows what they see or why they jerk their heads, as if repeatedly shocked, switching between the eye on one side to the eye on the other, thinking one thought at a time. If the animals see him, it will not matter because they will not interfere.

He hopes, once invisible, to begin his great work, a tapestry woven of nothing. Nothing but watching.

He will see and see and see, he thinks, and do nothing, neither add to nor subtract from anyone's life. He will watch everything he can—the odd shuffling of feet along crowded streets, men and women taking off and putting on their clothes, leaves falling and disappearing into gutters. He will stand still and silent in the corners of bathrooms and watch what people do when they are most certain that no one is watching. He will study the faces of mothers and fathers—which are never alike—as they wrench with fear for their children, and fear of their children. He will study children's faces as they greedily swallow love or try, sickened, to spit it back up.

He will try to see as much as an invisible man has time to see, and he will try to remember it all.

When he is done, when his eyes fail or he no longer has the patience or interest to continue watching, he will sit down and replay what he has seen in his head, becoming an invisible repository of invisible memories of bygone times, or of moments that threaten to repeat themselves for all eternity, which will be as much good to the world as anything else.

THE LINE

It's a small thing, a minuscule happiness, but something none-theless: the sound of my pen scratching across a page. It won't bring out the sun, I know, nor cure any disease or sorrow, but it's something, one thing, of which I can be sure.

For now, I am still content with the letters and words I drag behind my hand, but I am still young and there is more still-to-be-done than done. No doubt, when I have exhausted most of its possibilities, I will grow bored of "writing" as I know it now.

Some nights, when sleep is slow in coming, I have another thought: a dream, a fantasy, a faint hope that someday I will be able to drive my pen *into* the very surface of the paper, through it even, as through sea or sky, and draw a line toward a horizon ahead, and when I reach it, I will draw the line still further and further on. I will follow that line until there is no next thing.

THE VOICES

When a voice within him is ferocious in its torment, another voice answers, as if to comfort, saying, "though you do nothing now that helps anyone else, nothing that eases suffering in any way, nothing that brings anyone any form of joy, you would do what was needed, if a need arose and presented itself clearly, and that alone proves your worth."

Often as not, another voice rejoins: "It is in fact *because* you do nothing that you bring joy to others. You already practice the greatest of virtues for a man of your kind: silence and inaction. For you are, at heart, a bumbler, and would only do harm if you tried to help."

And then a third voice responds: "It is true that you are right not to help, but not because your help is not needed, nor because your help would harm. You know, at the core of your lonely heart, that your kind of help would be the most selfish: you would only help in order to feel helpful, because then you would think you proved your worth. And so, if you were for once to make yourself useful, you would ultimately only add more evil to a world so full of evil that there is no use for yours."

And all the while, as he is lost in thought, houses are burning with children trapped inside; flood waters are drowning entire cities; widows are wailing over lost men. Who will help them? Surely it will not be him.

Who will rise up, for mustn't someone? Who can tell the voices that call for help from those that only call to hear other voices call in return? Perhaps it is you. And perhaps not.

THE LAST

Only one tree remains. On the tree's one branch there is one leaf. Held by a thread, it is loosened by the wind like a child's tooth.

When the leaf finally falls, this particular act of subtraction will be finished. Then it will be time to turn our attention to the next.

There is a last thing for every moment, said the last sage.

Each thing does nothing more than await its turn to be last, said the sage that came after him.

THE WOLVES

Wolves rule these woods. They have overthrown the old rulers, conquered all the creatures, and now these woods belong to them.

But do not be afraid if you pass this way. There is nothing here that can harm you, because, of course, the wolves are made of something less than air.

Their bite is like a breeze. When they run a few leaves shake. Perhaps a flower bends when they howl.

Pass through the woods whenever you like. What you have to fear is not in the woods.

THE WIND

I have no secrets to keep. When I blow by, the trees and the rocks and the walls hear what you hear—I have no hidden language for them that you cannot understand.

There is only my breath, its force or gentle touch against whatever resists it: walls or windows, woods or rocks, creatures with their heads bowed, men holding their hats. There is only my breath, my voice.

Sometimes it is as soft as a nighttime whisper, and soon I am asleep again.

When it is a fierce, raging bellow, beware: I have no love then, no care for anything. I'll thrash whatever is in my way.

Sometimes my voice rages and then calms, rising from nothing, ending in nothing. That is a story you know.

Sometimes my voice is as sharp as the blade that could pierce your heart. I mourn myself, like you do, for whatever blows is always blowing away.

Do not be fooled—you know better than anyone what I mean when I speak; I need not dress my breath in words.

THE CHANGING TIMES

There is not much to say now, though of course there never was. Whatever was said was just a repetition, perhaps a slight rephrasing, of something someone already said, as this is, and as whatever is said after this will be. No one is fooling anyone, though that does not stop most people from pretending they're fooled, because pretending feels much better. Even if no one now feels much better than anyone ever did. It's not even hard for anyone to think things are different. In fact, the most amazing thing is how easy it is to think anything at all.

THE DUST

It is well known though little discussed that the dust, which collects in balls in corners, under beds and chairs, and in closets, is in fact alive. True, it is sedentary, silent, and anything but lively, but it has its own kind of life nontheless.

Like so much else that we willingly forget with age, the life of the dust is the secret province of children, who often care for particular clumps as pets. Of course, the dust, which will outlive all our future generations, adaptable as it is, really has no preference for, nor loyalty to, anyone. It is simply waiting for us to join it.

THE NEXT BOOK

There has never been much agreement among scholars, zealots, and hopefuls whose prayers rise quietly into the cool night air. After the writing of the first book, uncountable volumes of commentary and interpretation followed. Over the centuries it seemed every bellowing voice and studious supplicant contributed his book to a library that grew so vast and contrary that no building, country, language nor race of men could house it.

The books themselves seemed to battle one another, screaming back and forth across the long and difficult years. Because of what was written, more knowledge was lost than anyone could hope to record. In defense of books, men were sent to wars from which they would not return. Nations were founded and toppled because of what was or was not written. Millions died as the books weighed heavily on bowing shelves.

Books were burned and brittle fragments of charred pages blew like brown leaves in the wind, coming to rest in children's soft hands. Some children believed the few decipherable words were shameful secrets and destroyed them right away. Some brought the bits of paper home to their mothers and fathers, who hastily took them, commanding their children to forget, or hung the scraps on walls in precious frames. Other children secreted the words away in the darkest part of their hearts, which were already filling with fear.

And who can say for certain, what may, what already has, come of them?

II. from *The Book of Fear*

THE VIRTUES OF BIRDS

Two birds came upon a crust of bread lying on the path through the woods.

"Please, after you," said the first bird.

"No, you saw the crust before I did, you eat first," replied the second.

"No I didn't. I was distracted for a moment by a beautiful song. I thought it was a she-bird singing. I thought she might be calling me. But I could not see her among the trees. Then I saw you leaning over this crust of bread. So in fact you must have seen it first."

"I too heard singing, but I thought it came from over there, by the stream. I was about to walk that way when I noticed you on the path, guarding the crust."

"No, I was never guarding it. As soon as I saw you with the crust, I thought, 'there is plenty here for two birds—we shall both have a feast, if only you will not keep all for yourself.'"

"How could you think I would eat it all? I am only one bird, with room in my stomach for only half a crust of bread. When I saw you with your crust, I hoped you would feel the same way."

The sun was starting to set. The woods began to darken. The birds could hear a frightful clamor rising in the distance— grunting and shuffling in the leaves.

"Please," said the first bird, who sensed the darkness welling around him, "eat now—we haven't much time."

"Yes, it is growing dark," said the second bird, who remembered what he had been told about the woods, "but I would be impolite if I ate first, and politeness is foremost among the virtues of birds."

"Certainly it is," rejoined the first. "A bird hates to clutter a path on which someone is walking, so he skips away. But, for a bird, perhaps caution is a greater virtue. How do I know the crust is not laced with some poison to which you were a party. How can I be sure that you do not wish me dead so you can scavenge my nest for sticks?"

"Persistence is also a virtue of birds," replied the second coarsely. "How do I know that you do not hope to scare me off with your theories of poison and have the whole crust for yourself? And how do I know that you have not struck a bargain with a wolf or some other desperate animal. He may be waiting behind that rock right now, ready to swallow me whole."

"Go see for yourself. No wolf waits there," said the first bird.

"Ha! And leave you to make off with the unprotected crust! I think not," said the second.

By now it had grown terribly dark, and the creatures who haunt the woods were awake. The clamor closed in like a gloved hand slowly tightening its fingers.

SHADOW

She had a dog. She called him Shadow. He was not too small, but not too big. He could sit in her lap, but he was not so delicate that she couldn't play with him, when he wanted to play, which he often did, when he didn't want to eat, or sleep, or simply rest and watch things passing outside the window.

She knew that in the morning, Shadow liked to go outside and then have something to eat. Then Shadow would nap, and then want to play for a little while. Then Shadow liked to spend afternoons by the window. All in all, he was lovable because a routine grew around him on which a pleasant, orderly life could be based.

Shadow was a very predictable dog—except for when he saw his shadow.

It's tempting to think that this is how Shadow got his name, but of course she named him for his dark fur. Sometimes, too, it is tempting to believe that when something is named it grows to answer for the name it is given, to fill it out, to express the name in action, but this was also not the case with Shadow, for when the dog saw his shadow—and he did not see it often, for despite all the things dogs notice that people do not, there are other things dogs hardly ever see—something very surprising happened.

When Shadow saw his shadow, he grew very still, as if all his muscles had suddenly turned to stone, and slowly but surely, his shadow would begin to creep away from him. The shadow would creep slowly away and walk along the floor, flat as a shadow, while the dog stood frozen. The shadow would move like this until it reached the wall, then disappear into the crack where the wall and floor met. Then Shadow, the dog, would finally settle down, and usually fall asleep. When he woke, she thought he sometimes looked a little sad, like he looked when she left the house in the morning. But soon he would cheer up, and maybe want to go outside or play or just sit before the window, watching whatever passed.

And whenever this happened, she had the same thought: perhaps this is a sign; perhaps it is some kind of metaphor sent from wherever metaphors are born.

And perhaps it was, though she never knew what it could mean. For as surely as many strange things happen—things, which, because they are too unlikely or sometimes too horrible, cannot be believed—it is not given to us to know their meaning. Though someone must know—someone or something must. Mustn't that be true?

THE MONK AND THE STUMP

An old monk, who was returning from his last pilgrimage to the holy spring, sat to rest on a wide, withered stump near the path through the woods. As he rose to continue his journey home, he heard a gravelly cough and then someone saying, "Wait!"

"Who's there?" said the monk. "Who spoke?"

"It was I," said the stump, "the stump upon whom you've been sitting. Don't go. I am lonely, and you are the first guest I've had in many long years. The other trees will no longer talk to me. They say I'm somber and remind them of death."

The monk was a kind and thoughtful man, who, all his life, had tried to help whoever he could.

"I will stay for a moment," said the monk as he sat back down, "but then I must go, for it's getting late, and I'm old."

"Thank you," said the stump, "but why must you go? I've stayed here all my long life, and it's not so bad, if you have someone to talk to. Stay here and talk to me. We'll pass the time together."

"No, I cannot stay. I must bring this jug of holy water back to my monastery. I don't have long to live, and I wish to die amongst my brothers, who will ease my passing," said the monk.

"You don't need to leave. I'm sure someone else can bring your friends water. And what could be more easeful than these beautiful woods? Stay here and die with me. I cannot have much more time left either," said the stump.

"I'm truly grateful, friend, for your company and for the rest you've given me," said the monk, "but I really must be on my way. My brothers will worry. I'm sure someone else will come along soon," said the monk, who began to rise from his seat.

"You must stay!" rasped the stump. "I've been too lonely for far too long and I will not let you go! You see what they have done to me—cut down my beautiful trunk and taken my crown of leaves! They left me here to rot in shame!" the stump bellowed.

Now the monk was truly afraid and tried to run as fast as he could, but, being old and clumsy, he stumbled over one of the stump's thick roots and fell to the ground, crumbling his brittle bones. Then the stump began to knit its roots around him. They rose from the ground and coiled like snakes, pulling the monk into the earth until his mouth was full of soil, which muffled all his cries.

Night fell again over the lonely stump. In the morning the sun rose high, and birdsong echoed from the treetops.

RAISED BY WOLVES

He could have been, though he was not. He had never even seen a wolf—he had lived with his father and mother in a big white house with a bay window. But, had he been left in the woods—though they would never have left him anywhere, and never went in the woods—wolves could have found him, and instead of thrashing him about until he was only something for them to eat, they could have taken him in as one of their own, though, of course, this is not what happened.

Though had it happened, he would never have had to suffer his father's senseless midnight rages, nor his anxious morning silence, as though the day had been haunting him all night long, nor his mother's cowed protectiveness, all of which he did suffer, swaddled in a silence of his own. But he could have learned to detect the unfamiliar scent of an intruder in the woods, or the well-known odor of an enemy. He could have known how to distinguish predator from prey by the rustling of the leaves. Though what would prey on a wolf?

Of course, he never had to answer that question, for he was safe in his house, where even the walls cast shadows and the floors groaned to mark the slow passing of his long childhood years.

But he could have run with the pack—perhaps he could have even led it, were he able to tame his fellow wolves by filling their hearts with fear, which they deeply love, for fear brings order to their wild lives, tells them where to go and what to do. For he did know that those whom he most feared, and those whom he tried to make most afraid, were the ones whose love he most deeply needed.

THE LONG JOURNEY

Matthew had always lived in a small village to the south of the mountains. He had never traveled far beyond the edge of the village—perhaps into the neighboring pastures and meadows, but never much farther than that. When he was still a boy, a traveler had passed through the village. Matthew's father had told Matthew to call him Uncle Martin, and that is what Matthew had called him. Uncle Martin was a strange man with strange habits who was certainly not a citizen of the village. He drank from muddy streams and could talk to horses. But he had told Matthew wondrous tales of journeys he had taken to cities and villages far on the other side of the mountains. Though it had been years since Uncle Martin had appeared in the village, Matthew never forgot those tales. Matthew longed to embark upon a journey of his own, and now that he was sixteen years old, he felt the time had come.

One morning, soon after Matthew had made his decision, he went to his father, who was busy in the barn, and told him his plans: "Father, I am going to embark upon a long journey to the cities and villages beyond the mountains. I feel restless here, and my soul longs for wide open spaces and strange adventures," said Matthew.

"In fact, I agree, my son," said his father, which was not the response Matthew was expecting. "There is a whole world beyond this village. It will do you good to see it. And I have heard that in the cities beyond the mountains, they pay a high price for a calf from our side of the mountains, so you must take our calf on your journey and see if you can trade it for gold."

"Alright, father, I will take the calf, and I will bring back whatever gold I can get," said Matthew, as he looped a rope around the calf's neck.

News of Matthew's journey spread through the village. It seemed to await him wherever he went. Pulling the calf behind him, he stopped at the baker's to buy a few loaves of bread for his adventure. The baker was already excited when Matthew reached the door of his shop. "Hello, young adventurer," said the baker to Matthew. "I hear you are planning a journey to the other side of the mountains. Let me give you these two loaves of bread to take on your journey. They should taste good for days. Take them," said the baker.

"Thank you," said Matthew.

"But, also, I hear that they pay a high price in the towns on the way to the mountains for the cakes that we bake here. Will you take these three cakes, which I have wrapped for safe keeping, and see if you can trade them for gold? It seems a fair trade for the loaves I have given you," said the baker.

"Alright, baker, I'll try to sell the cakes, and I will bring back whatever gold I can get," replied Matthew, who carefully put the loaves and cakes in his satchel and made his way down the road with the calf.

Next he stopped at the tailor's, from whom he hoped to procure a new set of traveling pants. The tailor, of course, was eager to see him. "Hello, young wayfarer," said the tailor to Matthew. "I hear you are bound for the cities beyond the mountains."

"Yes," said Matthew, "and I've come here to buy a pair of traveling pants."

"Of course," said the tailor, "you'll need a good pair of pants, and I have just the pair. Take these," said the tailor, pulling a pair of well-worn, brown pants from behind his counter. "My son wore these when he took a similar journey, but now that he is married and lives in the village, he no longer has any need for them. I'll give them to you," said the tailor.

"Thank you," said Matthew.

"Only, I have a favor to ask," said the tailor. "I hear that they pay a high price in the cities on the other side of the mountain for the kinds of blankets we make on our side. Would you take one with you and see if you can sell it? That seems a fair enough trade for a pair of pants," said the tailor.

"Alright," said Matthew, "I'll take the blanket and bring back whatever gold I can get." Matthew folded the blanket and tied it with a rope to the calf's back.

Everywhere Matthew went to gather supplies for his journey, people in the village were eager to give him what he needed, and always asked that he take something to sell in return. The next morning, when Matthew was ready to leave, the poor calf was heavily burdened with cakes and blankets and scarves and hats, and Matthew's satchel was nearly bursting with trinkets and buttons and pots and pans, all the things the people of the village had heard would fetch a high price other cities and towns. As the sun rose, Matthew waved goodbye to his father and mother and set out along the road that lead over the mountains, with the calf following close behind.

By the time the sun was high in the sky, the village was far behind him and the mountains loomed larger than ever before. He had been told it would take two days to cross over the mountains and arrive at the nearest city on the other side. That did not seem like such a long journey to Matthew, but he hoped to sell some of his cargo and to continue walking to more distant cities. At midday, Matthew stopped for a rest. He tied the calf to a small tree and sat down on a stone.

Just then, a traveler came walking around a bend in the road. "Hello, young man," said the traveler.

"Hello," said Matthew. "Have you come from the city just over the mountain?" he asked.

"Oh, no," said the traveler. "No one is going to or coming from there. Haven't you heard? There's a war going on. The city is ravaged by merciless soldiers."

"Oh," said Matthew, "that's terrible news. I am on my way there right now, and I hope to sell this calf and these goods, to see the world, and then to bring back some gold for the people in my village."

"Well, the city over the mountains is no place to go. You'll want to try the town over the river instead. Head east at the crossroads and keep walking for two more days."

"Thank you," said Matthew. "That's just what I'll do." With that, the traveler went on his way, and Matthew stood up, untied the calf, and set out for the crossroads, which was an hour or two down the road.

When he arrived at the crossroads, Matthew was tired, and the poor calf was more tired still. The sun was beginning to set and it was time to rest for the night. At the crossroads was an inn run by an old woman who had seen countless travelers come this way. Matthew entered the inn and found the old woman at work in the kitchen. "Hello," said Matthew. "I was hoping I could find a room for the night."

"Yes, I have a room," said the old woman. Are you the young man who is bound for the town beyond the river?" It seemed that somehow, news of Matthew's journey had preceded him.

"Yes," said Matthew. "I hope to sell this calf and some of these goods, and then to see the world and bring back some gold to the people of my village."

"Well," replied the old woman, "you won't want to visit the town over the river. There is famine there, and sickness. No one comes from or goes there now."

"Oh," said Matthew, "that's terrible news. I had planned to go to the city just over the mountain, but found out it is plagued by war. If I can't cross the river either, where on earth shall I go?"

"You'll want to head southeast," said the old woman. "There is a village there where I'm sure you'll find what you're looking for."

Matthew slept at the inn for the night, and in the morning he set off to the southeast, tugging the tired calf behind him. As Matthew continued his journey, things went much the same way. Everywhere he stopped, someone told him to alter his course. He was now days and days from his own village. Perhaps it was weeks, or even months. He had sold or traded all that he had in order to buy food or a place to sleep. Even the calf had been sold to a butcher.

Without any gold, Matthew would be ashamed to return to his village, if he could ever find it again. But every day his journey grew longer. The world was vast and wide and strange. At every turn was something unexpected, a roadblock or a path that led through the woods. He crossed a dozen mountains and a dozen rivers. He stopped in towns and cities. No one could say Matthew hadn't had his adventure. And no one did say it. In each village or town or city where Matthew stopped, he told stories to the people he met of the places he'd been. Children's eyes grew wide as he told his tales. Some day, they thought, they would take a long journey of their own. They would cross mountains and rivers and meet strange people along the way. They whispered to each other about Uncle Matthew and pretended to get lost on familiar roads.

THE LUCK OF THE NAMELESS

He had never had a name. Of course, people always called him one thing or another, but he had never felt like any of those words was *his* name. He did not think he knew his name, nor had he ever heard it spoken aloud.

But perhaps he had heard it in his thoughts, the fanciful wonderings that flickered and dissolved, never again to resume exactly the same form, like smoke drifting toward the sun. Yes— he remembered, in a dream perhaps, having heard a name he recognized once or twice, though he could not now recall its sound or shape.

One day, lonely and nameless, he decided to set about finding his name. He began by making lists of all the names he knew. When the lists had grown long and fruitless, he realized that if he did not know his name, he would not find it among the names known to him. Yet if he had heard it in a dream, it must be there somewhere in the darkness of his mind.

For a long time, he thought about how he could both know something and not know it. Was his name, then, part of the knowledge of his body, like the way he knew how to clasp his fingers around a hunk of bread then draw it to his mouth and chew, though he could never explain how he did it, how the command to eat had been dispatched and obeyed? Or was there knowledge of some other kind—hazy forms, like the shapes of poems waiting for their subjects to fill them? But all this thinking brought him no closer to finding his name.

He wondered if perhaps other people knew it—if, somehow, his name was written, in lettering he could not read, on his face for others to see. For a long time, he asked everyone who would listen whether they could tell him his name. Some thought he was joking, and others were sure he was mad. A few played along, offering names—*You are John; Glory is your name; I will call you Joshua*—but none of the names was his.

Could he be the only one without a name? Did all the others feel safe and happy with the names they were given? Impossible. Then were they all hiding a secret name that only they knew, one which referred only to them? A name is only a word, he thought. How could it summon a whole person?

Each night he slept and dreamt and perhaps even dreamt his name one or two more times. Over the long years, he decided there was no name for him. At least not here, where names are tossed atop everything, like blankets, which leave everyone cold when they are withdrawn, as, inevitably, they will be.

In fact, he was lucky, he told himself. There was at least one humiliation he would not have to suffer: no one can hide beneath a name forever.

The Mountain Village

High in the mountains there is a village. No one from the village has ever climbed down the mountain, and no one not born in the village has ever climbed the mountain to visit. The people who live there believe that below the blanket of fog that skirts the mountain there is nothing but a black sea out of which a few mountains rise. Snake-like creatures of astounding size live in the sea; the villagers believe the snakes are the pets of their god, who sits on a throne beneath the waves.

The villagers' myths tell of the misery and boredom of their god, of how, many ages ago, he loved a goddess who spurned him and went to live in the sky.

The god tried to follow her, they say. He climbed high into the mountains, but the sky was even higher than the mountaintops. Looking out into the universe, the god did not see the goddess, and so he began to cry.

From his tears sprang the village, so the myths say, and the green places where the villagers grow their food and put their animals out to graze. As the god, in his despair, slid down the mountain, his tears became the blanket of fog, and soon the tears filled the basin of the earth and rose up around the god, becoming the black sea of tears in which the god now lives.

All the villagers' rituals and rites are rites of mourning, and when one of the villagers dies, they throw the body below the blanket of fog to feed the pets of their poor, sad god.

At the base of the mountain is another village. Those who live there never climb the mountain, atop whose foggy peak, their legends say, their goddess lives.

The priestesses of this village tell how their goddess was spurned by a bitter sea god, who lives in the waters below. When their goddess cries, her tears make the lands around the village green and fertile.

When one of these villagers dies, they plant the body deep in the earth, and they believe that when their goddess cries upon the bodies of their dead, trees spring up, their branches reaching for the heavens, their roots straining toward the god in the sea.

And so, most things can be explained when one knows that there are many villages and many mountains, many seas and many gods, who have loved and been spurned and do not dare to love again.

THE BURNING HOUSE

He was outside chopping wood when the blaze took hold of the house. He was standing some hundred feet away—a safe distance, far enough to escape the flames—when the fire rose from within and began consuming the wooden walls and then the roof. He had his back to the house, busy with his work, and so he did not see or hear the first flames growing. No, by the time he turned around, it was already too late to save the house.

Of course, his wife was still inside. She had just closed her eyes for a late morning nap—she was tired and a little bit sick—and a fire had been set in the fireplace to warm her. When the fire seized on some straw nearby, then hungrily spread from rug to curtain to chair to wall, she was thick with sleep.

You may be wondering what he did next. Did he run into the burning house to save his wife, whom he loved as much as most husbands love most wives? Was he already too late? Perhaps, if he ran back inside, he would find his wife dead and he would die in the fire too. Did he run away? Did he drop to his knees and wail unto heaven? Is it true, as is said, that a bird in the hand is better than two in the bush? Or, is it even possible that, beneath the inward cries of his dreams and fears, he was happy to be rid of his wife, finally free to choose a new life, a new name, a new fate?

These are all very pressing questions, and there are many more that could be asked. Perhaps, someday, we will find answers amongst the rubble.

But you must be wondering, too, whether now, while the fire rages, we should waste our time with questions. But if we fail to ask now, when will we? Isn't one of our houses always aflame?

THE UNEXCEPTIONAL BIRD

The day the little bird was born, no bells rang to mark its birth. When, many weeks later, the bird leapt from a branch and flew through the air for the very first time, no festival was held in its honor, though, to the bird, this certainly seemed a momentous occasion.

"I guess I'm not very special," thought the bird, "for otherwise someone would watch and mark my achievements. I must be—though I did not until now believe I was—one of god's unexceptional creations, like the grains of sand and the blades of grass, which, taken together mean a very great deal (for what would the world be if there were no birds? How could children dream of flight without our example to guide their dreams?), but as individuals they do not come to much.

Somewhat saddened, though reasonably satisfied, by this explanation, the bird went on about its life, eating unexceptional worms and gathering unexceptional sticks to fortify its unexceptional nest.

Then, one day perhaps a year later, the bird died when a squirrel accidentally dropped a heavy nut on the bird's head from high atop a tree. The squirrel did not notice, and most of the creatures in the woods were used to seeing dead birds, so no one said or thought much about it.

That afternoon, which was a warm spring afternoon, two children—a brother and sister who were known for having nasty manners—came walking through the woods on the path where it happened that the bird's body had fallen.

"Ho! Look!" said the brother when he came upon the dead bird on the path. "A dead bird, and freshly dead! What shall we do with it, sister dear?"

"Oh!" said this sister, who was very excited. "We must do something, for to leave the bird here would surely be a waste. Let us put it in this box I've brought," she said.

"Yes," replied the brother, "and then let us set the box on fire!"

"Wonderful!" cried his mischievous sister, "and then we can watch the bird pop and turn black like a loaf overcooked in the oven!"

And that is just what they did. If only the poor bird could have seen himself now. How truly exceptional he had become, at least to these two wicked children, who had never burned a bird before, and who had never seen one burned, on a lovely spring afternoon.

III. from *The Book of Sleep*

THE ROOM

Though it was always the same room, and he was always the same man, the room was always changing. Every time he looked around, it was different than the last time he looked. Every time he woke from sleep to see the room again, it was different than when he had closed his eyes. Every time he left and returned, the room had ever so slightly revised itself.

The changes were small, sometimes all but invisible to anyone whose eyes were not attuned. Sometimes they were actually invisible—there was no way to perceive or accurately describe them, but he always knew: the westward window suddenly faced more to the west. The large desk was infinitesimally larger. The hips of the nude statue in the corner were ever so slightly shapelier.

For a time, he tried to make his guests aware of these changes—"don't you see," he said, "how the fireplace has begun to swallow the floor? And come here and feel this blanket," he begged, "it's warmer than yesterday." But they never understood. They gave him queer looks and began to decline his invitations, which, after a time, he stopped extending.

He spent most of his days now alone in the room, watching it, hoping to catch it in the act of changing. But, always, no matter how he concentrated, the changes would take place behind his back—they had already happened by the time he noticed them: the door was shut tighter, the sunrise slanted through the windows at a more dramatic angle, the chair had altered its shape and was no longer quite comfortable.

How long had it been like this: the man in the room, the room always changing? He had always thought he was the same man, the room always the same room. Had the mirror changed too? How? When? He could no longer quite recognize the face he saw reflected in it. Somehow this face looked less like his and more like someone else's—like the face of a man who had spent a long time alone in the same room, which he believed was always quietly changing.

Who was this man? he wondered. Would there still be time enough to know him?

THE ORIGIN OF UNHAPPINESS

Now it seems obvious that there should be as many gods as there are words. But, before, when there was but one language and only a few people to speak it, the uncountable number of name-less gods—who were still awaiting their worshippers and their worshippers' words—was a source of great confusion, mostly to the gods themselves. Who should have power over what? Where was each god's domain?

One day, all the gods decided to meet in order to divide the heavens and the earth between them. So many gods gathered that they filled the heavens and crowded the earth. Many were forced to stand in the seas and even to gather in the place be-tween the heavens and the earth.

Soon, the impatient, uncomfortable gods began to argue. There were many who said, *I am the god of thunder*, and many who claimed to rule the land of the dead. Dozens of gods be-lieved they were the sole spirit of each river and lake. A thousand gods seemed to claim each grain of sand.

For days and months and years—before they were called days and months and years—the gods argued and fought. The sky and the earth and the water flashed and shook and roiled.

All the while, the few people multiplied and were happy speaking their one language and always understanding each other. One god saw this and was furious. Why, he wondered, should people, who are mortal and not nearly as powerful as the gods, be happy while the gods were prisoners to misery and confusion?

With a blinding flash of light, this great god gave each per-son a different tongue, a tongue which spoke different words from every other. Husband and wife could no longer whisper their secrets. Father and son shouted back and forth, uncomprehending. Friends bellowed at each other, collapsing under the weight of wasted speech. Some of the people spoke words similar enough that they could make out each other's general meaning, but even the same word never meant quite the same thing to two different people.

The people, who had, until now, lived in harmony throughout the earth, began to divide into tribes and claim certain parts of the world for themselves and for only those others whose words sounded the same. They fought and killed in the name of their words, hoarding the lands that they named.

This made the gods very happy—now they could share the sky and the earth and the waters, which the people had given as many names as the many gods—though the people were never happy again.

THE SUN

You know why the sun must rise in the morning, because, were it not to rise, the earth would always be cold and dark and joyless.

You know too why the moon must rise in the night, because, were the sun to stay in the sky, fear would be forced to hide in the shadows. It would never be allowed to roam the earth, to seep between cracks in the walls and into dreams and nighttime thoughts, as it does under the eye of the moon.

Then those who thrive on fear would also be forced into the shadows. There, they would do their dark work, as if it were night. And then, you know, all the rest—everyone else—would soon go into the shadows to join them, to partake of the dark work they do.

Soon they would all be afraid of the sun, which makes no place for fear and its breed. Everyone would live in the shadows, which welcome all who are afraid.

THE DRAGON

In fact, real dragons were quite small. They did breath fire, but only enough to be mistaken for a firefly on a very dark night. They were as harmless as fireflies, though that did not stop anyone from killing them.

THE CITY

In the city, there is a famous bakery where anyone with a little money can procure cakes and breads of the finest quality. And then, anyone with a little more money, and who knows the right question to ask the baker, will be led into the back room behind the kitchen, where the baker keeps his most special creations: cookies and cakes which look more like weathered stones or gnarled things dredged up from the sea, but which possess unusual powers. These pastries, ugly though they may be, can infinitely extend life, cure the direst illness, and even erase a person, and all memory of that person, from the face of the earth. This baker is an unusual man indeed, but this is not his story.

In the rooms above the bakery lives a woman who does not look particularly old, though she has lived in those rooms for as long as anyone can remember. There, she spends all day knitting, which is what everyone remembers she has always done. And when a child in the city turns nine years old, he or she is sent to visit the woman, who gives the child a scarf. Some of these scarves are of unspeakable beauty, and some are as plain and rough as the dirty back of a yew. But, somewhere in the home of everyone who grew up in the city, one of these unusual gifts can be found. Some wear them day in and day out, and some lock them away. But everyone, old or young, has a scarf knitted by this ageless woman, though this is not her story either.

On one particular day, a stranger was seen passing the bakery and the windows of the knitting woman's rooms. No one had ever seen him before. Where had he come from? Why was he here? People who said they had seen him tried to describe him to each other, and to people who said they had not. He was not quite handsome, but certainly not ugly. His clothes looked rugged, but certainly not poor. He wore an odd cap, they all agreed, with a large feather stuck in the brim, the kind of hat a rich man might wear, or a ranger. Who was this man? What did he want? Some people were sure they had seen him that day walking through the city streets, or rubbing the muzzle of a tethered horse, or down on his knees speaking to children in a language that only children know. Others thought they saw a man with a feathered cap, but then, perhaps, they did not. Perhaps, their curiosity excited to such a degree, they had imagined seeing the man and his cap weaving through the crowded alleys. Without a doubt, this singular man left his mark on the city, though, to be sure, this story is not about him.

Perhaps this is the story of someone still to come, or someone who has always been here but whom no one ever notices. Perhaps it is a story no one has ever told, or one told so often no one thinks of it as a story any longer. It could be a story that has yet to begin, or one so long past that it has been forgotten. Perhaps the story is still going on, and until it ends, no one knows how to tell it.

A ZEN STORY

The master was sitting beneath a tree counting gold coins. The student came to him and said, "Master, we have renounced all worldly possessions—why do you count these coins like a miser?"

"How can I renounce what I do not know I have?" said the master, looking up at the student.

Understanding his master, the student sat down beside him and began to count the leaves on the tree, the blades of grass on the ground, the birds in the sky, the clouds, the stones, the drops of water, his fingers, his toes, his feet, his legs, his hands, his arms, his torso, his mouth, his nose, his ears, and his eyes. He counted his friends and his enemies, his mother, his father, his many brothers. He counted his wishes and woes, his dreams, all his thoughts, and then he was gone.

THE FIRST FIRE

The very first fire burned for an hour. It seemed to set itself ablaze and then it ran its course. The second fire burned for a day, the third for a year, and so on, until the fire burned longer than anyone could measure.

Men threw their food into the fire, and still the fire burned. They threw their cattle into the fire, and still the fire burned. They threw their wives and daughters and sons into the fire, but still the fire burned.

The fire burned the land and the sea, swallowing houses, forests, islands, even the water, which burned and burned and burned.

Soon all the men were gone, swallowed by the fire. The animals were also gone, and the plants, all of them swallowed by the fire. The fire threatened to swallow the whole of the earth, which was now little more than a glowing coal at the tireless fire's core.

There are many stories of fire, but all of them end in the same way: as inexplicably as it had burned, the fire cooled and smoldered and finally went out, as if anything else could happen.

THE CROW

The crow was not always a crow.

A long time ago, before anyone knew how to count the days, or noticed how much time was passing, most men lived for hundreds of years. Eventually, when a man grew tired of being a man, he walked down a long road until he was only a black speck in the distance. Anyone watching would see the black speck suddenly take flight, a black bird joining other black birds in the sky.

More recently, most men have fallen in love with time, have come to love it more than anything. They await the day of their death like a holiday, crossing off the minutes, the days, and the years from the moment they're born. Too busy counting down to nothing, no one has the time to walk down long roads anymore.

Now when a man dies he falls to the ground, into a hole, and soon becomes the dirt that covers him. And crows are just crows; men watch the invisible hours instead, which fly away and never return.

THE STORY OF THE STONE

When the first frost settles over everything, you find you have become a stone. When it grows colder all around you, and things begin to huddle together for warmth, you are only as cold as you were when you first became a stone.

When everything is buried in snow—the trees up to their waists, all the brown leaves on the ground, the burrows and the creatures who live in them—you are only as buried as you were when you first became a stone.

When the world begins to grow warm again, and the ice thaws, soaking the earth with water, you thaw only as much as you thawed when you first became a stone.

When it is finally warm everywhere, and life is buzzing like the bees who anoint every new flower pushing up to claim its life, you claim only as much life as you claimed when you first became a stone.

When great heat beats down like a thousand fists upon the world, and everything is sluggish, sulking like sweat across the grass, you sulk only as much as you sulked when you first became a stone.

And when everything begins to die—when the leaves and the grass and the streams wither and turn brown—you die only as much as you died when you first became a stone.

THE RED CIPHER

It's wrong to think of it as a bird. True, it has wings and a beak, but so do many things, in one way or another. And it does have feathers, but don't be hoodwinked by those. There are also the usual twigs and worms and eggs, but in its nest, if you know where and how to look, you will find something else no bird possesses: the red cipher's little book of accounts.

Only two or three of these books have ever actually been smuggled out of the deep woods, but according to those who have seen them, they are truly astounding. Either because it was commanded to do so by some force of nature, or because it found that keeping infinitesimally detailed accounts was a mysterious key to its survival, the cipher evolved the almost unfathomable capacity to write—in the comfort of its otherwise ordinary nest—the most unlikely and unique book in the world.

Like those unusual houses that are much bigger inside than their exteriors suggest, the cipher's book of accounts has no discernable beginning or end. The lucky few who have seen a book report that it contains the most meticulous records of each and every thing that happened to every creature on the earth, written in every conceivable language.

Some who have read the books have even found entries pertaining to themselves, mostly composed of facts that should have long ago been lost to oblivion: the weight of a spoonful of soup from a bowl eaten two decades ago, or a tally of the falling leaves they've seen.

It is impossible to know why, let alone how, the cipher came to possess or compose its unusual book, or how it has come to know, if indeed it does "know," the information therein. As might be expected, there are some who believe that within these mythical little books can be found the answers to man's most fundamental questions. Others swear the answers can be found in a book kept by another creature altogether, one that closely resembles a turtle. Still others insist that the answer to the question of where the answers can be found is one more secret to be sought.

A WALK

Death and Birth went walking together, eager to play.

"What shall we do today?" said Death.

"Let's give life to something new," said Birth.

"Alright," said Death, "but tomorrow, let's take it away."

"Okay," said Birth, "it would never work if we did it the other way."

THE BONEMAN

The Boneman comes to town busily rattling his bones. He comes one day a year, and no one knows what day it will be, though it is usually after the last autumn leaves have fallen. Whether this is because he must visit other towns at other times no one can say. The slightest mention of the Boneman in other towns is always met with the queerest look, but whether this is because everyone believes the Boneman is his own town's private puzzle or because no one else has heard of him no one is sure.

No one can agree on what the Boneman wants when he comes to town. Some believe he comes to sell his bones, which a few—mostly the old—believe act as charms against illness and bad luck. Indeed, some have approached him and come away with bones, which apparently he is willing to sell, but no one remembers hearing him advertise that he has come to sell or buy anything. Others say he travels the country gathering bones, which he adds to a hoard he stores in his home, wherever that may be. Some have spoken of him scouring the trash piles and digging in places where dogs are buried. Still others insist he is no more than a crazed vagabond who wanders in search of who-knows-what.

No matter the truth, he always comes, and has done so for a long, long time. Some even think of him as a kind of marker in the year, saying things like, "the Boneman has come—it is time to bring out the winter wool." A few phrases like this have been passed down and allow us to recognize those whose families once lived in our town.

In many ways, the Boneman is as beloved as he is feared, a proud secret to some—like a flirtation with another's wife—and a dark shame to others, like the memory of having tortured and killed a cat as a child. We do all know, or at least we believe, that there are some things which must occur and which we cannot understand. Without them, the world would surely stop.

TIME

I was once a bigger stone, and I'll be smaller stones soon enough, says the stone. I grow only in number, never in size. Time will never make a mountain, but it made each grain of sand.

\-

You will never find my source, nor my final drop, says the river. I am always on my way between. Time flows like a finger that never narrows to point, yet never widens to join a hand.

\-

What you hear has always just ended, or is always about to begin, says the song. Music is what is between silence and sound. Time is the work of a band.

\-

I am what the sun shows, but what you won't show the sun, says the shadow. Yet I am gone at night. Time is what takes away whatever you understand.

\-

I stop where the sky begins, yet never touch what I grow to reach, says the tree. I am a living wish. Time ends each sentence with *and.*

ACKNOWLEDGMENTS

Thanks first to Peter Conners of BOA Editions for making a home for this book, and for his patient and generous responses to my unending questions. Thanks to everyone at BOA—I'm so grateful. Thanks to Jesse Ball, for inspiration, friendship, and encouragement. Thanks to Amanda Stern, for getting excited about these pieces at their very beginning. Thanks to Jonny Segura, for being a real fiction writer. Thanks to W.S. Merwin, for *Houses and Travelers*. Thanks to Richard Howard—it's prose, not prose poetry, I swear, though may it be prose that reverses. Thanks to Aimee Bender. Thanks to Matthea Harvey, for your kind words and for dressing this book so stunningly. Thanks to Brenda, thanks to Brenda, thanks to Brenda. And Thanks to Cal, for making sure the story always changes.

And a very big thank you to the MacDowell Colony, a real place out of myth, where this book got its start and a bit of its world.

I would also like to thank the editors of the publications in which some of these pieces first appeared, sometimes in slightly different versions:

A Public Space: "The Virtues of Birds"
Conduit: "The Burning House," "The Unexceptional Bird"
Double Room: "The Wind," "A Walk"
Fairy Tale Review: "The City"
Jubilat: "The Wolves"
LIT: "The Changing Times," "The Room"
Paraspheres 2: "The Luck of the Nameless," "The Origin of Unhappiness," "The Mountain Village," "The Next Book," "The Dust," "The Line"
Pleiades: "The Monk and the Stump"
Post Road: "The Groaning Cows," "The Story of the Stone"
Virginia Quarterly Review: "The Prisoner," "The First Fire," "Raised by Wolves"

ABOUT THE AUTHOR

Craig Morgan Teicher is the author of *Brenda Is in the Room and Other Poems,* which was selected by Paul Hoover for the 2007 Colorado Prize for Poetry. His poems and criticism appear widely. He teaches at several universities and also works in publishing. He lives in Brooklyn with his wife and son.

BOA Editions, Ltd.

American Reader Series

No. 1 *Christmas at the Four Corners of the Earth*
Prose by Blaise Cendrars
Translated by Bertrand Mathieu

No. 2 *Pig Notes & Dumb Music: Prose on Poetry*
By William Heyen

No. 3 *After-Images: Autobiographical Sketches*
By W. D. Snodgrass

No. 4 *Walking Light: Memoirs and Essays on Poetry*
By Stephen Dunn

No. 5 *To Sound Like Yourself: Essays on Poetry*
By W. D. Snodgrass

No. 6 *You Alone Are Real to Me: Remembering Rainer Maria Rilke*
By Lou Andreas-Salomé

No. 7 *Breaking the Alabaster Jar: Conversations with Li-Young Lee*
Edited by Earl G. Ingersoll

No. 8 *I Carry A Hammer In My Pocket For Occasions Such As These*
By Anthony Tognazzini

No. 9 *Unlucky Lucky Days*
By Daniel Grandbois

No. 10 *Glass Grapes and Other Stories*
By Martha Ronk

No. 11 *Meat Eaters & Plant Eaters*
By Jessica Treat

No. 12 *On the Winding Stair*
By Joanna Howard

No. 13 *Cradle Book*
By Craig Morgan Teicher

COLOPHON

Cradle Book, by Craig Morgan Teicher is set in Adobe Garamond which is based on roman types cut by Jean Jannon in 1615. Jannon followed the designs of Claude Garamond which had been cut in the previous century.

The publication of this book is made possible, in part, by the following individuals:

Anonymous

Aaron & Lara Black

Gwen & Gary Conners

Mark & Karen Conners

Charles & Barbara Coté in memory of Charlie Coté Jr.

Peter & Suzanne Durant

Heidi Friederich

Kip & Debby Hale

Janice N. Harrington & Robert Dale Parker

Bob & Willy Hursh

Robin, Hollon & Casey Hursh in memory of Peter Hursh

X.J. & Dorothy M. Kennedy

Elissa & Ernie Orlando

Boo Poulin

Steven O. Russell & Phyllis Rifkin-Russell

Vicki & Richard Schwartz

Ellen Wallack

Rob & Lee Ward

Pat & Mike Wilder

Glenn & Helen William